What is phonics?

Phonics helps children learn to read and write by teaching them the letter sounds (known as phonemes), rather than the letter names, e.g. the sound that 'c' makes rather than its alphabetic name. They then learn how to blend the sounds: the process of saying the sounds in a word or 'sounding out' and then blending them together to make the word, for example c – a – t = cat. Once the phonemes and the skill of blending are learnt, children can tackle reading any phonetically decodable word they come across, even ones they don't know, with confidence and success.

However, there are of course many words in the English language that aren't phonetically decodable, e.g. if a child gets stuck on 'the' it doesn't help if they sound it out and blend it. We call these 'tricky words' and they are just taught as words that are so 'tricky' that children have to learn to recognise them by sight.

How do phonic readers work?

Phonic reading books are written especially for children who are beginning to learn phonics at nursery or school, and support any programme being used by providing plenty of practice as children develop the skills of decoding and blending. By targeting specific phonemes and tricky words, increasing in difficulty, they ensure systematic progression with reading.

Because phonic readers are primarily decodable – aside from the target tricky words which need to be learnt, children should be able to read the books with real assurance and accomplishment.

Big Cat phonic readers:
The Singing Beetle

In Big Cat phonic readers the specific phonemes and tricky words being focussed on are highlighted here in these notes, so that you can be clear about what your child's learning and what they need to practise.

While reading at home together, there are all sorts of fun additional games you can play to help your child practise those phonemes and tricky words, which can be a nice way to familiarise yourselves with them before reading, or remind you of them after you've finished. In *The Singing Beetle*, for example:

- the focus phonemes are ee (beetle), i-e (like), a-e (snake), ea (treat), oo (looking), ie (tried). Why not write them down and encourage your child to practise saying the sounds as you point to them in a random order. This is called 'Speed Sounds' and as you get faster and faster with your pointing, it encourages your child to say them as quickly as possible. You can try reversing the roles, so that you have a practice too!

- the tricky words are 'all', 'her', 'she', 'was', 'said', 'want(ed)', 'I', 'little' and 'want(s)'. You can play 'Hide and Seek' by asking your child to close their eyes and count to 10, while you write each word on a piece of paper, hiding them somewhere in the room you're in or the garden for your child to find. As they find each one, they should try reading and spelling the word out.

Reading together

- Have a look at the front cover of *The Singing Beetle* and talk about what you can see.

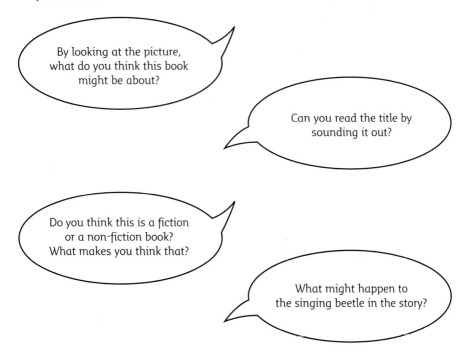

By looking at the picture, what do you think this book might be about?

Can you read the title by sounding it out?

Do you think this is a fiction or a non-fiction book? What makes you think that?

What might happen to the singing beetle in the story?

- Enjoy reading *The Singing Beetle* together, noticing the focus phonemes (ee, i-e, a-e, ea, oo, ie) and tricky words (all, her, she, was, said, want(ed), I, little, want(s)). It's useful to point to each word as your child reads, and encouraging to give them lots of praise as they go.

- If your child gets stuck on a word, and it's phonetically decodable, encourage them to sound it out. You can practise blending by saying the sounds aloud a few times, getting quicker and quicker. If they still can't read it, tell them the word and move on.

Talking about the book

- Use the story map on pp18–19 to retell the story together, remembering what happens to Poppy and Harry the mouse.

- Practise the focus phonemes from *The Singing Beetle* by asking your child to find specific words with, for example, the 'oo' phoneme, or sounding out some of the key words, for example 'treat'.

The Singing Beetle

Written by Linda Strachan
Illustrated by Oliver Hurst

Collins

Poppy the beetle liked to sing.
She sang all day.
She sang if she was happy.
She sang if she was sad.

Squeak!
Squeal!
Screech!

The rest of the beetles didn't
like Poppy's singing.
They said her singing
was squeaky.
No one wanted to play
with Poppy.

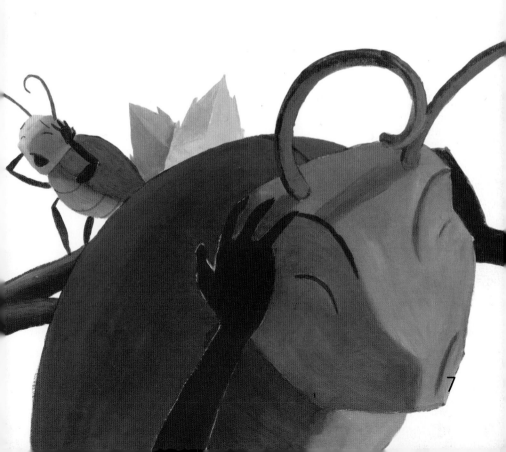

Poppy was sad. She went off
into the woods.
"Now I can sing as loudly as
I want!" she said.
She sang so loudly that ...

8

… she didn't spot Harry,
the mouse!
Harry was looking for a treat.

Jake, the snake, was looking
for a treat, too.
"Yummy, a mouse!" he said.

But Poppy's singing was
so loud ... that Harry didn't
spot Jake.

Jake looked at Harry.
Harry looked at Poppy.
Poppy looked at Jake.
"Look out, little mouse!"
Poppy cried.
"A sneaky snake wants you
as a snack."

Harry got a fright.
"A snake!" he said.
He ran to hide in a heap
of leaves.
He tried not to shake.

Jake's tummy gave a rumble.
He went to look for Harry.
"Look out!" said brave
little Poppy.

Then Poppy began to sing.
It was loud and squeaky.
Jake got a fright and
he slid away.

Harry came out.
"You are a brave beetle,"
he said.
"And I like your singing."
"Really?" said Poppy.

Harry liked to sing, too.
"We can sing together!"
he said.
So Harry and Poppy sang
together, every day.

Squeak!
Squeal!
Screech!

A story map

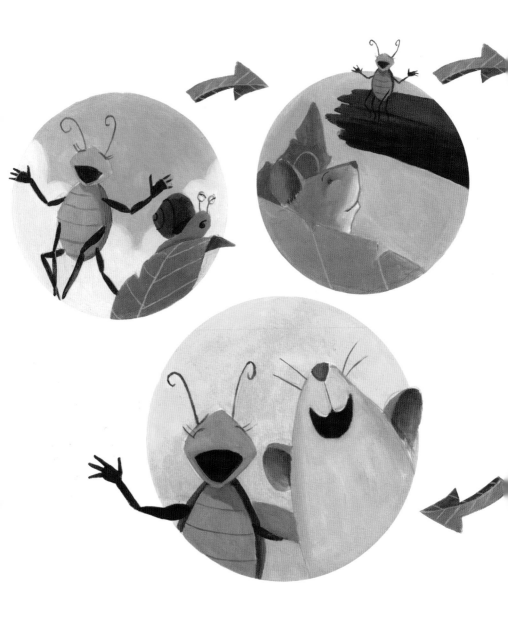

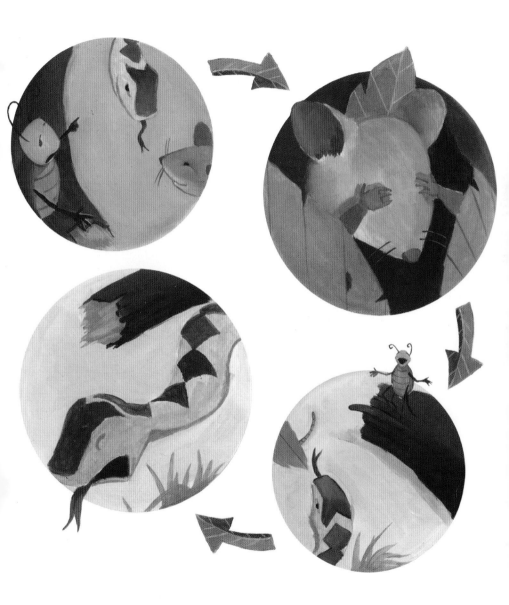

19

Getting creative

- Have some fun with your child by asking them to be a phoneme detective! Ask them to search the book for words that contain the 'ee' and 'ea' focus phonemes. Can they sort them into two lists?

- You could keep practising the tricky words by looking through some newspapers or magazines together and seeing if you can spot any letters that make up the tricky words, cutting them out and sticking them together to make words.

- If your child's enjoyed reading about the singing beetle, they might draw a picture of Poppy. They could add words to describe what she's like, e.g. brave, happy, lonely.

Other books at Level 2:

Fiction	Non-fiction
Zog and Zebra — Mal Peet and Elspeth Graham, Sarah Horne	The Sun and the Moon — Paul Shipton
A Day Out — Petr Horáček	The Rainforest at Night — Nic Bishop
The Singing Beetle — Linda Strachan, Oliver Hurst	Gorillas — Teresa Heapy

Collins Big Cat
Reading Lions

Published by Collins
An imprint of HarperCollins*Publishers*
1 London Bridge Street
London
SE1 9GF

© HarperCollins*Publishers* Limited 2011
This edition was published in 2015.

Author: Linda Strachan

British Library Cataloguing in Publication Data
A catalogue record for this publication is available from the British Library.

Illustrator: Oliver Hurst
Designer: Nicola Kenwood, Hakoona Matata
Parent notes authors: Sue Reed and Liz Webster

Printed and bound by RR Donnelley APS

www.collins.co.uk/parents